Jasper's Beanstalk

Nick Butterworth and Mick Inkpen

Macmillan
McGraw-Hill

New York   Farmington

On Monday
Jasper found
a bean.

On Tuesday he planted it.

On Wednesday he watered it.

On Thursday
he dug and raked
and sprayed and
hoed it.

On Friday night he picked

up all the slugs and snails.

On Saturday he even mowed it!

On Sunday
Jasper waited
and waited
and waited...

When Monday
came around again
he dug it up.

"That bean
will never make
a beanstalk,"
said Jasper.

But a long long

long   time   later . . .

It did!

(It was on a Thursday, I think.)

Now Jasper is looking for giants!

Macmillan/McGraw-Hill

*A Division of The **McGraw·Hill** Companies*

Macmillan/McGraw-Hill
1221 Avenue of the Americas
New York, New York 10020

Printed in the United States of America

ISBN 0-02-181111-3 / 1, L. 2

4 5 6 7 8 9 SEC 02 01 00 99 98 97